V: WaveSon.nets/Losing

D1504793

Prizewinning poet Stephanie Strickland pushes the boundaries of the printed word to create an invertible volume, with two beginnings, that expands our traditional views of reading and experiencing poetry. From the undulant V-fold of the book's open center one jumps, via a Web site pointer, to V's third section, http://vniverse.com. V lives on the page, in electronic space, and between these two.

"Strickland's lyric poetry reads the entire gamut of knowledge—'from sails to satellites' and from shadows and spectres to spectral analysis—through the figure of Simone Weil, for whom knowledge of the spirit was to be attained by lived proof. Imagine this, and you will appreciate how a lyric poetry of such ethereal embodiment can be made to scintillate through hypertext, linked to lines of flight and seeming fantasy. Yet the really good news is that Strickland puts the lyric poem to the test as if, quite as much as music, it were the very instrumentality of a quickening mind."
—Marjorie Welish

"In V the poetics of Wittgenstein and Weil—quotidian, notational, mathematical, emotional—are revisited and re-formed. They are, in a word, saved. This is a truly modern book, a guide to the noetic spheres where we are obliged by history, science and heart to go. It is a thrilling work that is above all *useful*."   —Fanny Howe

"Stephanie Strickland is one of a handful of outstanding writers working to forge poetic forms at the intersection of technological innovation and the tradition of experimental writing. V is a networked artifact. As a double work, the book contrasts its own internal forms, its winged halves converging on a pivot / hinge from which it leaps toward the constellations of its Web extension. Product of an intellectual imagination similar to Simone Weil's, this poem is radical in integrating new technology, not as a novelty or special effect, but as a way of thinking."
—Johanna Drucker

"Stephanie Strickland's V is an experimental, philosophical poem, in part a mystical meditation on mathematics, in part a love poem to non-existence. Strickland uses a transgressive style of sentence and syntax and numbering to cross epistemological boundaries and to question worship of the ideal, while offering a new beauty in its stead."   —Brenda Hillman, from the Alice Fay Di Castagnola Award citation

STEPHANIE STRICKLAND is the author of three volumes of poetry and winner of several awards. Her work has appeared in such journals as *The Paris Review, Grand Street, Chain, The Iowa Review,* and *Ploughshares.* She has composed several prizewinning hypertexts, including *True North* and *The Ballad of Sand and Harry Soot.* She lives in New York.

ALSO BY
STEPHANIE STRICKLAND

Give the Body Back

The Red Virgin: A Poem of Simone Weil

True North

True North: Hypertext

V

LOSING L'UNA

STEPHANIE STRICKLAND

PENGUIN POETS

PENGUIN BOOKS

Published by the Penguin Group
Penguin Putnam Inc., 375 Hudson Street,
New York, New York 10014, U.S.A.
Penguin Books Ltd, 80 Strand,
London WC2R 0RL, England
Penguin Books Australia Ltd, 250 Camberwell Road, Camberwell,
Victoria 3124, Australia
Penguin Books Canada Ltd, 10 Alcorn Avenue,
Toronto, Ontario, Canada M4V 3B2
Penguin Books India (P) Ltd, 11 Community Centre, Panchsheel Park,
New Delhi - 110 017, India
Penguin Books (N.Z.) Ltd, Cnr Rosedale and Airborne Roads, Albany,
Auckland, New Zealand
Penguin Books (South Africa) (Pty) Ltd, 24 Sturdee Avenue,
Rosebank, Johannesburg 2196, South Africa

Penguin Books Ltd, Registered Offices:
Harmondsworth, Middlesex, England

First published in Penguin Books 2002

1 3 5 7 9 10 8 6 4 2

ISBN 0 14 20.0245 3
CIP data available

Cover Design by Talan Memmott
Cover Drawing by Guy Ottewell, *The Astronomical Companion*

Printed in the United States of America
Set in Centaur
Designed by M. Paul

A C K N O W L E D G M E N T S
V :   L O S I N G   L ' U N A

Barrow Street **3** 1999
"From Sails to Satellites" as "Advice From an Astronomer"
"Errand Upon Which We Came"
"TITA: The Incandescent Thought About"

Fence **8** Fall/Winter 2001/2002
"I Will Thread Thee"

Image: A Journal of the Arts and Religion **23** 1999
"Simone Demystifies Mercy"

Image: A Journal of the Arts and Religion **31** 2001
"Action at a Point"
"All Body"
"Superstition of Chronology"

Mid-American Review Fall 2002
"Imagination"

Samizdat **1** 1998
"Despite the Most Active Resistance"
"Lady and Her Family"

Seneca Review **XXX:2** 2000
"Essay on Mis-labeling"

For *Simone Weil,* her Life & Thought;

her need to touch;

her gut, her mouth.

V: LOSING L'UNA

V
LOSING L'UNA

1.1

In the "hell" hole of total brightness: no time.
Voluntary obedience: the most
profound

1.2

pleasure. It is pink
I see, red windows in my room. There are shadows, dappling
the screen from small, square-leaded panes

1.3

in the open casement. Late afternoon. See how the sun
has trained me
to wait, how I stop, look up,

1.4

into the soft stand of pine, the one spruce—
and it comes, it comes in flood, that angle of dying. Later,
today,

1.5

a little. It seems. Without
a clock, my whole body stops
to wait . . . .

1.6

An order
makes itself known, inside a lower, only by zeroes
or by zinnia seeds.

1.7

At school,
she is called—by her teacher—*The Martian.* To distinguish
her, from other

1.8

women,
called
"Corset-crushed Insects."

1.9

Freed,
the captive is wretched. It is wretched to recognize
as false what seemed

1.10

so good, so possible, so complete: vertigo,
nausea. To emerge
from the cave

1.11

with some knowledge, but not yet to know it,
until you un-dark-adapt, un-ark-
adapt, dissolve

1.12

into the luminous, the light that dapples
the eyes with dark dots. Do these mar
vision?

1.13

Advice
from an astronomer: avert
your eyes, look away

1.14

to see better,
to avoid
the blind spot hidden deep

1.15

in your seeing, the impassible blindness
of the entry
mark, the door of insertion

1.16

of the optic nerve, to enhance
your ability
to see near the threshold of what can

1.17

be seen. For something right
on the edge, try the blink method: first look away
from, then, directly at. What

1.18

appears, when you turn aside, disappears
when you look back. (*Thought,*
for its own

1.19

self-preservation, flees.) At the decisive
moment,
says she, it is by inert

1.20

things "the soul" is saved, daily: "the body," that powerful
instrument
of salvation, she said: body, the tether.

1.21

A body—a tether—is a small boat afloat
on a turbulent sea, that semblance of steering,
then it goes

1.22

belly up. Not simply to notice
the stars, not to register
the stars,

1.23

but to quiet
and open the mind to something
outside it: the whole of Greek

1.24

science. Attention: the whole
of Greek science, the profound correlation—to read
inert symbols, to become part

1.25

of the conversation that physical
truths enter into with
numbers. (Musical numbers, scores, patterns, algorithms . . .)

1.26

From Sails to Satellites, J.E.D. Williams, reviewed in *The Sciences*,
Jan/Feb 1994, p. 51:

> ". . . even Williams, who surely must derive comfort from the ease of
> contemporary navigational methods, senses that something has been lost
> with the passing of the sextant and the chronometer. Navigation has
> become a matter of numbers, whereas once it was a way of apprehending
> one's place in the cosmos. Williams recalls one long flight across the
> Atlantic, on which, plagued by radio failure, he was forced to shoot the
> stars to determine his flight path. Clouds stretched below him in an
> unbroken sheet, obscuring the marine light that would have marked the
> African coast. But, as Williams remembers, 'when we broke cloud and
> there was the light, exactly where it should have been, the sensation was
> more of harmony with the universe than satisfaction with oneself. A
> computer display is not the same thing.' "

1.27

A universe
meets the hand that pushes against it
in the form of

1.28

a limit
that it pushes up against, or seeks
to circumvent; it rewards

1.29

a hand-mind that reaches for
its breast, a mouth not
held back,

1.30

by pattern upon pattern giving way to deeper
grasp giving in to rhythm or
vibration or milk.

LOVERS

Lovers are never one.
Narcissus
is never two. Desiring

some thing
is
impossible: the true

desire
is for nothing. Into
nothing, only

nothing without ripple or
concussion,
can

desire *all-
absorbing* sink itself and always
sink.

2.31

I was going to say that heaven did not seem to be
my home; and I broke my heart with weeping
to come back to earth . . . .

2.32

A mind
is trapped, Miss Mary Mack, by number,
by the number of relations that can be simultaneously present,

2.33

while ignorant
of thoughts which involve a greater number: unformulable
thoughts,

2.34

though rigorously clear, each
one of the relations capable
of precise expression

2.35

in words.
(It is why we cling secretly to nonsense, runes,
the fairy stories. People

2.36

assume
that thinking does not pledge them—it, alone,
pledges.)

2.37

Spectator 435, July 19, 1712:
"It was very entertaining to me to see
them

2.38

dividing their speculations between jellies and stars
and making a sudden transition from the sun
to an apricot."

2.39

The Lady and her family, being the spectacle
of the *Spectator*, are perhaps conscious,
as they *simultaneously*

2.40

make jam
and read cosmology, of being
entertainment, and perhaps this does

2.41

affect them, in
their (great, formal, triple) task.
N-tble, Hentable, Mother Magree, the Lady's

2.42

pain
is
a formality.

ACTION AT A POINT

1

God, by force
by surprise and by appealing to greed,
tries to make the soul

2

eat a pomegranate seed. If the soul
allows but one
expression of consent

3

to be torn from it,
God wins. Simone, who abhors
coercion, in life,

4

in language
does not. When the soul
is given over, entirely,

5

God walks out
and leaves her, abandoned,
solitary.

6

End
of prologue. This is where
the story starts.

3.43

Cut the ring in half—she still insists
on the *roughness*
of the divide: "body," "body" slash

3.44

"what"?
What you jump at,
shy at. Bristle at.

3.45

Water's pliant attentiveness,
the negative trial: not to eat a fruit,
not pomegranate, not apple;

3.46

not to open a door,
nor the lid of a box, not to think
about the white bear, not to look

3.47

upon
him, naked;
Kore, Pandora, Psyche, Eve, Briar Red, Snow White,

3.48

what is infinite
in doing is don't
ever: the taboo, the *geas*.

3.49

Simone, when you leapt, angled barbs on the fence
tore your scalp and you kept
rubbing blood from your eyes and stared and wouldn't

3.50

lie down,
or when the branches you barged through flooded you
with petals, white, wet, more softness

3.51

than you could shake off, you gave
no ground. Tines of lightning split
the tree: inside, creamy

3.52

and yellow. Your eyes brightened only
as the storm shifted, colder, harder, less
lurid. A word

3.53

can drain your cheek.
The lips of your wound begin to mend, but heal badly,
a welt, discolored, brown

3.54

as dogwood petals knocked to the ground,
notched with crimson,
as if blood flecked the wind.

IMAGINATION

1

If a woman has to make
a violent effort
to behave as she would naturally be

2

expected to, this is,
you said, the void, an inner
tension to which nothing

3

corresponds.
Void.
Nothing. Better,

4

you said, than equilibrium
gained with the help of actual things;
better, by far, than equilibrium invented

5

by imagination. *Imagination does not cease
blocking up the cracks
through which grace might enter.*

4.55

Assured, or cocksure? Astounding, her
severity of judgment. Preaching
neither love nor virtue, she traded in money,

4.56

ration books, coal, lodging, instruction, help
with job-seeking, passports, citizenship
& testimony.

4.57

A paralyzing deep-seated sense
of ineffectiveness coexists
with hyperactivity and apparent over-confidence, as

4.58

the clinical text says. Perhaps. But to learn
"they" come from *tight-knit*
non-fighting families prone to conflict-avoidance

4.59

and live out the remarks made about them . . . well,
some, maybe all, bodies resonate
to others' spoken words, but here, it seems,

4.60

words eaten. And re-heard. *The anorexic*
feels herself to be a victim
of nicknames, of wrong labeling.

4.61

To call Olbers' Paradox *Olbers'*
Paradox is wrong labeling. Miss Gingerbread
Dickinson is wrong labeling, unless we imagine her

4.62

indeed a witch, *maîtresse* of a sugar house
she baked which did not melt
around its own oven, sensing she must court

4.63

the children of the place. Stein
(as opposed to Gerty M.) barely able
to be labeled—as she engineered—

4.64

but a lot of "wrong" fluster and not
anorexic; so, perhaps, too *broad* a cause,
one must pause before relying on it.

4.65

*For an anorexic, an autonomous woman is
a contradiction in terms.* Whereas,
for Simone, "decisiveness" exists in the privileged

4.66

castes. Others come to see it as a truth and fact
of nature. And *she* came to see it, who knew
it wasn't so, temporarily immersed

4.67

in the work of those
others; she, too, eviscerated; entitlement lost
in a practice that occurred directly

4.68

on her body, scheduling her body. "Qualities
I thought my own, of my mind, were removed
inside one hour on the factory floor."

4.69

Why struggle to combat affliction?
In order, she answered, to restore the false
sense of a rightful self to every person

4.70

that they might make the only significant
choice open to them, *how* to renounce it
again, turn or not turn, leap—or stay; but since

4.71

it is the only choice, the only *human* thing,
the conditions of a full life being the same
for all human beings, our vocation

4.72

in the world *is* to restore the sense
of a rightful self to those deprived of it. To all,
that is. You and your partner, in every

4.73

interaction, restore,
or defeat.
Tertium non datur. Simone

4.74

was acute. Stein dark and sparkling. Money
was prominent in their writings,
and how wealth grows and families, and peoples,

4.75

and "pleasant family life," and one's native
language: roots of every sort. That knowledge
thrown up in a person kept apart, then

4.76

displaced, then again driven out—of her refugee
country, on her third reversal of fortune,
and so forth. Weil advised De Gaulle

4.77

to free Algeria: Antigone,
defeated, echoing Cassandra's wail—
our firebrand brother, Paris,

4.78

burns us all. *Aii-eeee!*
she said, do you know with *whom*
you deal? Or the stake? Or *how* they are called?

SIMONE DEMYSTIFIES MERCY

1

Helping someone, not to be obliged to think
about them anymore, or for the pleasure
of feeling how far

2

from them, how far from that, you
are: ordinary
charity *is a form of cruelty.*

3

To feel,
the soul must divide: one point in it
impassible, proof against

4

contagion; all the rest polluted
—to an extreme—
by the swollen heart

5

breaking. Mercy is
strained, nailed between two poles.
It is easier

6

for us to feel pity,
mixed with horror
& repulsion.

TITA: THE INCANDESCENT THOUGHT ABOUT

5.79

As the reed, torn from its roots
and cut to a flute whose whole song is longing, so too
the heart, made to be broken. Consent

5.80

to be broken is difficult
to give, for we imagine
ourselves

5.81

either powerful or powerless. Passion
forgets
the beloved, life, superdense

5.82

globular clusters, dispersing universe and the stars
it harbors, a nuclear forge
in the carried along scattering fall, multiversical

5.83

clones—or open clusters
like the Pleiades, the motion of a starfish
arm. Isomorphic?

5.84

Very like. Very
like
what?

5.85

GNOSIS 2: *These are the numbers relating to time*—
By the waters of Babylon I sat down.
Cuneiform, an assembler language

5.86

made to master cumbersome number.
I saw children who would be servants,
I saw children worshipping sequence.

5.87

It was nothing to them to reproduce
2000 lines of error-free code to make
a monkey laugh on the phosphorescent glass.

5.88

In 14 days the moon was dead. Times 2,
it grew again. Times 13 months, it made
364 days—plus one seed.

5.89

GNOSIS 1: *These are the solids relating to Godde.*
Pyramid, black, compact crystal of Heat
in the Octahedral Air.

5.90

Water, an Icosahedron sparkling, a near-
Sphere
swallowing the Kube of earth.

5.91

Sky, always in 12 parts, Docadecahedron.
These are the stones
of the Celts, of the Etruscans.

5.92

GNOSIS 3: *Cantor dusts, Devil's staircase, a gallery of monsters?*
Or, a museum of science and the comfort that offers?
Or wind, and the way the hole seems to keep moving.

5.93

Now the rueful, the serious work
of building bridges, finding
methods that are no more than stories

5.94

inserted in the world at a singular
point—the winged horse Buraq made of breath
and mounted on his back,

5.95

Arcing Iris, whom I see but cannot touch.
There is a doubt not incompatible
with faith—these truths

5.96

true so long as we don't think them that become false
as soon as we do:
at the moment

5.97

the liar thinks, *I am
a liar,*
she is not.

5.98

What must be kept
profoundly secret
—from ourselves—things true until we think them.

WEARING OUT

1

Your canvas shoes wore out. You refused
to buy others. So when Thibon
got you work

2

in the arbor, somebody gave you
old sabots.
The strap gnawed your ankle.

3

You kept pace. Never behind
by a single plant. "Pluck!"
the harvest-master said.

4

World at war.
Glasses.
Shoes.

DESPITE THE MOST ACTIVE
RESISTANCE

6.99

Does it leave you cold
if mass and sound
share the same signature, a simple one, a sine wave?

6.100

A sine, a rippling curve, the ink
on a pendulum, or tuning fork, but deeper now,
or finer-meshed, what signature of light?

6.101

We, adrift in the midst of mathematical
revolution
that refuses to understand itself.

6.102

In this sudden possession neither my sense
nor my imagination
had any part; I only felt . . . the presence

6.103

of a love, like that which one can read
in the smile
on a . . . face. As she said,

6.104

nothing . . . happened. As she said, *You*
cannot communicate anything to me
except yourself.

6.105

"Patriarchal Poetry": to love and to reject
the language and literature in which you write—
"Letter to a Priest":

6.106

love, reject,
the faith by which you live.
In common:

6.107

a secret, plain way of speaking
like the purloined letter—
apprehensive in love, because a sword

6.108

hangs over: one woman
smiles, that one is stately. That one
is heavy-bodied and she feels light.

6.109

This one is thin and feels
clumsy. Each of them, tokens,
trained with males, Harvard's Annex,

6.110

Henri Quatre. Bring the self-
castrating old men, bring Tolstoi,
bring Gandhi, to stand

6.111

beside them—barren women, not
made bitter, not shocked,
not unable to work, not mesmerized

6.112

by ruin: Simone Weil,
"On the Right Use of School Studies,"
Gertrude Stein, *Mrs. Reynolds.*

SUPERSTITION OF CHRONOLOGY

1

The Mysteries,
regarded as sacraments, may have been
Sacraments, a same virtue from a same relation to

2

the Passion of Christ: then to come;
today, past. The historic and the imminent, everything
in time equidistant from that hanging: hung from it.

3

How could a *chronologic*
fact
have a determining role, in this, a relationship between G[o]d

4

and souls, one term of which is eternal, not touching time,
except
once *where everything is zero, where the axes of the Cross*

7.113

Gentle Reader, begin anywhere. Skip anything. This text
is framed
fully for the purposes of skipping. Of course,

7.114

it can
be read straight through, but this is not a better reading,
not a better life. You are being asked

7.115

to move with great
rapidity. As if it weren't there. As if you were a frog,
a frog that since it's disappearing

7.116

thinks to ask,
for the first time, in which element it really does
belong. Leaping progress

7.117

will consist
in considering this and closing the book. Anything
else will represent a settled course.

7.118

Indeed, it is true that much has fallen
through the cracks,
but the most painstaking and willful path

7.119

will not recover this (recoverable?)
material any better
at all than the soft ziggy sampling butterfly approach.

7.120

Gentle Reader,
who labors, who tugs up roots to get beyond roots
——as it were——do roots entwingle

7.121

space? Where do we mine that knowledge
of what cannot be precipitous, nor yet
delayed?

7.122

What if the go(o)ds refuse
to go
to market? What then?

7.123

Will is broken by the trials of all folktales, the Augean stables,
the straw spun. A nail
that fixes the center so the register is true—

7.124

what the scale hangs on,
not what
the pointer points to.

EVIL IS EXTERNAL

1

Evil is external to itself: where it is, it is not felt.
It is felt where it is not: the feeling
of evil is not

2

evil.
Where it is: the God-blaming criminal;
where it is not:

3

a woman
feeling in her body what the rapist denies,
denies hoarding, denies passing on, because

4

he does not feel it. She
feels it. The whole weight of his force
and his forgetfulness;

5

it stops with her. It stops her.
No one wants to see it. To see it is against
the soul's

6

aspiration, *ergo* she is beaten.
Or killed—
or stoned or shunned.

8.125

Her
last spoken
word, *nurses.*

8.126

God cannot, Godde
can only
introduce some silence, hear;

8.127

God cannot, Godde can only
make the world
porous;

8.128

Godde l[ac]una[e] [l]um[en] losse
intervalle itervalle maykth
a May makyr [im]maculat[e] . . .

8.129

Acts of restraint restrayed, acts of re-nun-
ciation on Godde's part, Godde not a Self-Expansion,
seriating stopless,

8.130

but, O, a withdrawal, a make room, expand expend, expend
all—O . . pening inward where n . . O space was, O . . nly folded
walls. Godde-and-all-Godde's-children

8.131

less
—a loss—
than Godde-

8.132

Alone.
To percolate all things—to be hidden
in the dark,

8.133

unable
to be hurried, absconded, away, in drag, to masquerade
as light.

8.134

Do we need to recapitulate, recatapult, here, have we gone on
too long without a theme. I will thread
thee th[m]emes:

8.135

Prodigal Expenditure. Bankruptcy. Decreation. Withdrawal.
Grit.
Presence: Vale of Sensations of. *Value* of Sensations of.

A slide from Will to Willingness.
Manual Labor.
Far from holy the firm, full of holes the Intact.

Testing: Flesh the Sieve.
True Treasury the Trove of Mathematical Metaphor.
Strongly preferred: sense-soaked geometric to algebraic kites.

What the criminal doesn't feel is crime.
Standing with the ruled.
All paths are not equal. All equally have paths.

A need for insanity, for recognition, for mediation: 3 faces of (lo)ve.

[*Sieve of what is real in thought, as matter*
tests propositions in science, the part played by
the living body of the worker

which is essentially mysterious.]
St. John *poiountes aletheian* to do
the truth.

8.136

The Pharaoh's Breastplate.
Lops of memory.
Mandelbrot: *A different central limit theorem*——

8.137

And Ladysmocks all silverwhite,
mode[l]s vs. Description, will you call it In-completion
or call it Ab-undance?

8.138

And there is pansies, Johnny Jump-Ups to us,
carpet of hearts-ease, rosemary
for grace,

8.139

rue for remembrance.
"Simples" hanging from a nail
in my grammar's kitchen sweeten

8.140

the pot or salve a wound; when witches use,
bewitch then clove, wormwood, Artemisia, lambswool,
love-in-idleness.

8.141

Characteristics of text: such old notes.
Uncited quotes. Circling alternating movement,
the fireligisci genre,

8.142

the scireligifi genre, fragments
sans either shore or ruin. Old shire rain, or
shared runes, rather, roans, rowans, ripe cherry ripe.

REASON

1

The voice of reason
is an act
of the will,

2

furtive in regard
to itself,
to no longer know what

3

I have set apart,
to no longer
want

4

to know—
a spill
. . . of milk.

L'UNA LOSES

0.0

Moon over Manhattan.
Moon over Dover.
Moon over

0.1

the London-Dover train,
over bed 104, almost at the intersection
of two wings,

0.2

moon over the meadows
of St. Jean de Lalandes
where she had pitched hay,

0.3

over Carron de Gron
where she worked
beetroot fields,

0.4

St. Julien-de-Peyrolas
whose grapes
she had picked stretched out on the ground.

0.5

The danger not
that I should doubt whether there is
any bread, but that, by a lie,

0.6

I should persuade myself that I am not hungry.
It was a different set of wars.
Configuration is not statement.

0.7

The invisible pole, although she does not
write it—only twice
referring to it,

0.8

boats unloading at the dock—that would be 1942.
Reciting another's text. One pole.
And the other, Jardin du Luxembourg.

0.9

Another's text: *Taste my meat.*
Occupation: *Rédacteur (C.F.N.L.)*
Religion: too ill

to be examined properly.
Weight on admission:
stretcher case.

The painful struggle
about her light began all over
again. L'una eaten by night,

by sun, by war,
by the sequence of events in an ordeal,
or quest,

yet what did she seek? *The reality*
my inattentiveness
screened. Now sinking

all the time.
But soon I will no longer be
cut out.

0.9

To deny the opposition, "good" slash "evil,"
she said, use Irreligion: no difference between them—
or Idolatry, force supersedes

0.8

them; a third
way, to mute this opposition
occurs in the Gospels,

0.7

a way of living based on obligation, a concrete
way
of placing the body, grounding

0.6

violent
apprenticeship—
Tuesday

0.5

night.
At half-past ten.
Loss, she said, is the heart

0.4

of gambling.
L'una
loses. Luminous, lingering, dropping

0.3

her net, her cut
spool of star-
stained ocean, Channel foam, the Roman

0.2

sea, cliffs of Manhattan.
I will be added and united.
Failing, falling

0.1

behind,
below, inside, the crashing, faintly
smoking surf, she

0.0

fades
to day, to dawn, to
gone, to Dis-

o

appeared.

ALL BODY

1

All body
        washed through
by the soul. All soul

2

secreted
by the body.
                Al jabr:

3

to bind, to set bones, to name the unknown
as such—
        to worship a sign;

4

geo–
        metrein: to move, to measure
in the sand, to reason from your hands, to remember

5

the route
        the sign has come; to till
or to steer, to dowse, or to kill,

6

       to count, to scar, to make mine,
or to find
something not myself.

V

http://vniverse.com

There Is a Woman in a Conical Hat

V

http://vniverse.com

There Is a Woman in a Conical Hat

V: WaveSon.nets/Losing L'una

Prizewinning poet Stephanie Strickland pushes the boundaries of the printed word to create an invertible volume, with two beginnings, that expands our traditional views of reading and experiencing poetry. From the undulant V-fold of the book's open center one jumps, via a Web site pointer, to V's third section, http://vniverse.com. V lives on the page, in electronic space, and between these two.

"Strickland's lyric poetry reads the entire gamut of knowledge—'from sails to satellites' and from shadows and spectres to spectral analysis—through the figure of Simone Weil, for whom knowledge of the spirit was to be attained by lived proof. Imagine this, and you will appreciate how a lyric poetry of such ethereal embodiment can be made to scintillate through hypertext, linked to lines of flight and seeming fantasy. Yet the really good news is that Strickland puts the lyric poem to the test as if, quite as much as music, it were the very instrumentality of a quickening mind."
—Marjorie Welish

"In V the poetics of Wittgenstein and Weil—quotidian, notational, mathematical, emotional—are revisited and re-formed. They are, in a word, saved. This is a truly modern book, a guide to the noetic spheres where we are obliged by history, science and heart to go. It is a thrilling work that is above all *useful.*"   —Fanny Howe

"Stephanie Strickland is one of a handful of outstanding writers working to forge poetic forms at the intersection of technological innovation and the tradition of experimental writing. V is a networked artifact. As a double work, the book contrasts its own internal forms, its winged halves converging on a pivot / hinge from which it leaps toward the constellations of its Web extension. Product of an intellectual imagination similar to Simone Weil's, this poem is radical in integrating new technology, not as a novelty or special effect, but as a way of thinking."
—Johanna Drucker

"Stephanie Strickland's V is an experimental, philosophical poem, in part a mystical meditation on mathematics, in part a love poem to non-existence. Strickland uses a transgressive style of sentence and syntax and numbering to cross epistemological boundaries and to question worship of the ideal, while offering a new beauty in its stead."   —Brenda Hillman, from the Alice Fay Di Castagnola Award citation

STEPHANIE STRICKLAND is the author of three volumes of poetry and winner of several awards. Her work has appeared in such journals as *The Paris Review*, *Grand Street*, *Chain*, *The Iowa Review*, and *Ploughshares*. She has composed several prizewinning hypertexts, including *True North* and *The Ballad of Sand and Harry Soot*. She lives in New York.

V

WaveSon.nets

Stephanie Strickland

PENGUIN POETS

PENGUIN BOOKS
Published by the Penguin Group
Penguin Putnam Inc., 375 Hudson Street,
New York, New York 10014, U.S.A.
Penguin Books Ltd, 80 Strand,
London WC2R 0RL, England
Penguin Books Australia Ltd, 250 Camberwell Road, Camberwell,
Victoria 3124, Australia
Penguin Books Canada Ltd, 10 Alcorn Avenue,
Toronto, Ontario, Canada M4V 3B2
Penguin Books India (P) Ltd, 11 Community Centre, Panchsheel Park,
New Delhi - 110 017, India
Penguin Books (N.Z.) Ltd, Cnr Rosedale and Airborne Roads, Albany,
Auckland, New Zealand
Penguin Books (South Africa) (Pty) Ltd, 24 Sturdee Avenue,
Rosebank, Johannesburg 2196, South Africa

Penguin Books Ltd, Registered Offices:
Harmondsworth, Middlesex, England

First published in Penguin Books 2002

1   3   5   7   9   10   8   6   4   2

ISBN 0 14 20.0245 3
CIP data available

Cover Design by Talan Memmott
Cover Drawing by Guy Ottewell, *The Astronomical Companion*

Printed in the United States of America
Set in Centaur
Designed by M. Paul

ACKNOWLEDGMENTS
V : WAVESON.NETS

American Letters & Commentary **13** 2001
"WaveSon.net 40," "WaveSon.net 41"

Drunken Boat http://www.drunkenboat.com **2** Winter/Spring 2001
"WaveSon.net 19," "WaveSon.net 20," "WaveSon.net 21," "WaveSon.net 22"

Fence **2:1** 1999
"WaveSon.net 1," "WaveSon.net 2," and "WaveSon.net 3" as
"There Is a Woman in a Conical Hat" 1–5, 8–14

Grand Street **70** 2002
"WaveSon.net 32"

Harvard Review **22** Spring 2002
"WaveSon.net 28," "WaveSon.net 29," "WaveSon.net 30"

LIT **2** 2000
"WaveSon.net 4," "WaveSon.net 5," "WaveSon.net 6," and "WaveSon.net 7" as
"WavSon.net 4," "WavSon.net 5," "WavSon.net 6," "WavSon.net 7"

Meridian **6** 2000
"WaveSon.net 12," "WaveSon.net 13"

Notre Dame Review **11** Winter 2001
"WaveSon.net 14," "WaveSon.net 15," "WaveSon.net 16," "WaveSon.net 17,"
"WaveSon.net 18"

Notre Dame Review **12** Summer 2001
"WaveSon.net 23," "WaveSon.net 24," "WaveSon.net 25,"
"WaveSon.net 26," "WaveSon.net 27"

Ploughshares **27:1** 2001
"WaveSon.net 34," "WaveSon.net 35," "WaveSon.net 36," "WaveSon.net 37"

Poetry New York **12** 2001
"WaveSon.net 38"

Web Del Sol Editor's Picks http://webdelsol.com/f-epicks.htm Winter 2000
"WaveSon.net 8"

For *Simone Weil,* her *Life* & Thought;

her need to touch;

her gut, her mouth

V: WAVESON.NETS

WaveSon.nets 1–47

1–47

To go on / To go back

48

V

WaveSon.nets

WaveSon.net I

If you understand virginity,
you understand abstraction, you understand V—
V which is flight, and you understand VVV,
i.e., ric-rac, the earliest recorded

symbolic motif, Cassiopeian breasts pouring forth
a Milky Way, a.k.a. zigzag,
world-over water, meander, serpentine
cupmark U adjoining its inverse, upsidedown

U (please imagine), yourself
optimizing, as you do not lift but leave
your point (become pointed) pressed hard
to bone to pull that bone

writhing on your point, twist it one way,
then the other—a rhythm method making
your water mark.

If you understand red, you understand ruby,
you understand light bubbling up struck seam
first morning cliff; you do not
mock the real

as you watch it subside and divide and then run
like morning into the virtual.
If you understand vulva, you understand lens,
you understand an entrance

to unsuspected, fertile, labyrinthine darkness,
the power of ex-opponents or logs. If you put
your meander/zigzag/ric-rac
on your fabricated lens-shape, if indeed you dip

your lens into water and discover that the water
you meant to mark the lens with as a sign
of vulval moisture

is itself a lens, this clear drop beading up
on your lens stone, and you can see through it
to a life in the stone, to a depth
you did not suspect, do you bother to go back

to your old ox-head, its uterine face,
its Fallopian horns, to mark them
with meander, once you have discovered
wells open at the bottom leading to the next world,

wormholes, keyholes, the high
road to heaven, the flying carpet, the cataract?
You might. You might
go back,

stunned—for you no longer live
but rather remember what is a suddenly long-ago
childhood: marks

as marks, flesh as flesh,
their secrets those of separate realms.
Back then, a diagrammed
circuit *not* a circuit, as it is, now,

incised by the woman's, or the robotic,
"hand" on the golden wafer
in the virginally pure and guarded
clean room, eye to lens, as she makes her

—but whose?—meander mark.
If you understand virginity,
you understand abstraction and all there is to know
of immaculate, conception.

If you understood red, but—you cannot;
for you understand web
glistening in sunlight as stronger than steel

per ounce. You attempt to reverse engineer it,
as you once calibrated the magnification achieved
by a dewdrop, compelled,
and even soothed;

but if you understood ruby, the haunted road
of a human
voice, complex waveform,
not (by the ear) disassembled, not

processed in separate
recordings, followed on
by component reunitings, no *visual* mix, but all fused
into one

vibration received by one membrane,
the eardrum . . . porous . . . heard herald world
of word shaped.

When Columba converted the mermaid,
which of them said,
"Is it really
you?"

And then, after a time, who
replied, "How good is God's memory?"
Struggling to ward off being mounted,
since this would leave the chorus

without a conductor, and sensing a near-
lag in the beat, the man with too much state
in his head holds tempo,
pacing, tone, and volume constant,

but instructs the drummer (who is rarely, really
never, mounted) to vary
the breaks, to force possession

or reprieve it, techniques
to project
from psyche to physique
to psyche. A waltz

frames the mind of coquetry;
a tango, desolation.
That drummer in control during ritual
—but not of it;

that drummer in control during ceremony,
barely of it, has changed his name.
He plays Intendo on the virtual
causeway to the titular

see: he is a mystery fan.
Is it really you,
he longs to say, but I swim away,

repeating his beat, his cadence,
with my tail,
so opening a channel.
A channel only open, not a code, no

message, for him
to break. I fall away
from his design and say
to myself, so, we must meet apart

in a time
of no tomorrow, no pleading, no art,
time of waiting, a miracle mer-main
of hallucinated hearing.

Fin(-ger) to finger, I shiver,
am calm: the reef embraces the water
that wears it

down.
You have seen, with your own eyes, yes?
Or believed the lie that it can't
be lost, that it lives

somewhere else, somewhere safe
as it is not
in that slippery, silken twist
of cord

run by rhythm through psyche
to physique to sea to sky to water falling, dripping
with the sound of the water bird veering
on whose back

the earth rides.
Apprehended where every cell engaged: an entire body,
paralyzed, knees

drawn up, nails drawing blood,
neck rigid, tears streaming from shut
eyes, locked jaw, grinding teeth:
that silent song

possesses every
Erzulie, Her every *serviteur*, whose fragile
beauty, whose zephyr lilting lightness
has been tempered

by the cracking whip, by Petro fire,
Erzulie Ge-Rouge, who comes to the poor
in pink and white perfection, cologne
lavished from a faceted bottle and a swath of lace

down the skirt of her improvised dressing table,
she is almost Tennessee's
Blanche, whispering coquette, all

roses, shells, and smile,
until she starts to weep.
And cannot
be stopped, every cell engaged.

Is Tuesday her day? Rose her scent?
Titon
will tell you, you must feast her.
You must replenish

Source, would you keep her,
going back and forth, not as a footpath,
but a smile.
Not as a footpath, as a meal.

We do not eat to turn into food—food which we think
we can reach out and take,
but we cannot take what can only be given.

He now let the animals name *him*.
He played tag with them
and was vanquished by touch.
As she wove her seven-bristled,

quarter-circle broom,
as she told the days to parturition, did she curse
the most time-taking
way, the straight

path, the unaccelerated route?
Playing cat's
cradle with the V, wedging the gap,
corking

the grail, that bottle of time too soon
spilled out. Left to itself,
in tidal flows,

there would be no tomorrow.
She craves that drift.
But this is her
primordial

task, to keep time, to serve it, an order
learned from the water bird
who makes a 3-prong
Y print

in the sand, echoed each time she stands
in trembling waves.
A cast
shadow, a thrown reflection,

and a subtly bent refraction
where the water meets the sky
and the land, 3 axes, and a mapping,

and 5, she mapped, who veers
as she flies, who carries the tilted earth
on her back. This is hallucinated hearing
in the service of art, of Arthur's table,

R2, Artemis,
and Ursa guarding the Pole.
Welcome, then, Presence, Reflection, Shadow,
Refraction, She Who Stands,

Gnova, Gnomon, Goose, Ouzel, Orca, Longdark,
Hardware, Software, Wetware, a Dolphin
leaping, responding
to the bare boy on her back.

For a crown is a cradle.
Wings are conical baskets of grain, baskets of fish
slung from her shoulders.

She will apportion, determine, sustain
and guard,
Our She, if she keeps her cards going,
if she makes her pack,

if she burns the string figure holes in their backs,
peepholes to heaven, to check
on heaven and to check
heaven. If she serves

her mother, the Goose who is flying
into the gap, who uses
a hook, the hooked jaw of a salmon,
to tat, to get

from one side
to the other, a bird's only task
beyond keeping track,

a hook which appears
in the fourth year, the year
of its spawning,
the Year of its Leaping, dying, not eating, falling

apart as it travels up, flails
to breed.
Feel her power in bird or stone, or in her eyes
or breasts, alone, or even in

her hieroglyphs.
There is a woman in a conical hat.
When we chain her waist
with dice and cards,

a punished witch. The Jack of Knaves
comes up at 128, the one
who stole

her tart. She will sit
on a bird
or a broom. Or an axle-tree.
Or a mill wheel grinding.

She keeps time
timely, and you know her: Green, Great Circle, Noon.
My computer tells me
2:32

PM and so salutes her. Not P,
of course. Of courses, M
the *Maîtresse* (VV
reversed, please imagine), M the standard without which—

M not mother, but an anchorage, Anchoress, arbitrary
necessary prime first,
Royally

observed,
at the Green-wi( )ch
meridian.
A bee lives 28 days, that vaginal cadence,

nose swollen in honey.
The tree rings itself with another ring each year
and in its hollow live the bears—a world
tree closes. Major

and Minor, they circle the hole,
dipping honey from the hollow
at the tilted top
of the northern world, Polaris, star at the very end

of the Little Bear's tale.
To know
there is a pole, a polar axis to the earth,

and that it tilts. The thought
of such knowledge, hard to gain,
how to keep, we have lost,
except for the Rabbis who copy the Talmud,

who know by G[ ]d no scintilla
must change, not by unconscious slips,
not "corrected" by sages, not in 26,000 years—
me, I take what I get

from the Navy's lunar Web Page,
but I should go to Tarot: 52 weeks, 4 season
suites of 13 (moon-months, 14 x 2 days) [364] are not
enough: "a year and a day," [365] will (nearly)

fit the sun in, that's the Joker,
and in the Leap, fourth
Year, a year-and-a-day and *another*

day, then the long counts begin. After one-hundred
and twenty-eight
years, the need to take a day *out*—
as the osprey pulls a salmon from the sea

or the knave steals a tart. Penelope, star
undoer, keeps 128 suitors
at bay, while her husband cycles.
At Arthur's table, 128 Knights.

26,000 years
for the pole to "precess," to draw its circle
in the sky and return to the star
where it started out, while the Zodiac belt

slips backward through its signs.
2000 years ago we came
to the Age of Fishes, rising horizon at the vernal

equinox. But now arriving
at the Water Carrier, dare I mention
13 x 2000? Or the Tarot cards
in my Marseilles Deck,

my pocket calendar-calculator pack
that tracks the Platonic (the Precessional)
Great Year—a run-time,
portable version;

or my Wheel of (inevitable)
Fortune—that wedge, gap, joking Fool
at the top,
unnumbered, of no worth, holding all

together. So easy to forget,
to forget and conceive, to forget to turn
the card over, did I send a card

for Easter?
Original holes burned through to see
stars—who *are* those figures
(from an Ice Age? Neolithic?)

and what is the meaning
of the red bar?
(Do it over, upsidedown.) Rotate
and turn. 78

in all, my set compact.
All gods kill each other and all collapse,
except the horned. When, at last,
the King of Swords comes up, the Zodiac moves

one to the right, a complete Precession.
Insert Precession Day
and it moves back over, Crab again

in the middle, Crabs stabilizing Crosses
on the Grand Ellipse.
Little diamond-shaped double gaps
printed by a reindeer hoof.

And Lady with a heart-shaped face,
from 33,000
B.C.E., who knew the hidden
gate, that there is one, unknown

Joke as a tholepin of Creation,
gap. There is a Lady
in a conical hat. When we chain
her waist, when she hangs in a cage,

spread out, pinned up, in the market
place,
who

sees? Who but I,
sings
the bird: Sweeney in a tree, or Philomel,
or shepherds on the mountaintop.

Did Plato see?
Longing to say, *Is it really you?* All too
aware that the writing on his page
really wasn't, he heatedly forbade sung poems

of knowing in his *Republic*, even as he told
the old, the Orphic, the Egyptian, the lost
land undersea stories. The coast,
of course, had fallen

since the Ice Melt, the old shore now many miles
out. Though some escaped
to the offshore islands, or the Konya plain, and began

to imitate. Making a fake
from grotto to crypt, to the pre-final form
of stalactite and stalagmite, the Gothic cathedral,
to our Virtual CAVE™

Environment, in Illinois, where again we stage the Cosmic
Voyage to the Beginning—whose algorithm
this time?
Polished greenstone

double axes, a dying God
who had once returned intact:
in the beginning,
to stay alive and to leap from his back

between his horns. Then, not the bull
God, but the hunter returned.
Then not the hunter, but the hunter in pieces,

butchered, gored. Collected
by crazed women, crazed by the new thought,
the new
incompetence: to bring back a bull,

or ox, kill it, be killed
by it. Then in 14 pieces,
then 28, a moon-death,
for it was always, early

and always, about birth
and re-
birth. The child who went to the bull,
or to the dolphin, the girl

who became the hunter
was lured
from her task, or was it a boy, by the Titans,

the Giants, who offered toys: a top,
a mirror,
jointed dolls, knucklebone dice.
In the grave at Çatal Hüyük,

a bright blue neck,
green eyebrows on a skull—
are they wings of a bird?
Or a dragonfly in flight? Miniature

green stone axes
beside.
Metamorphosis
now morphosis, now

morphing: Matisse
repeating
that sea scene on a wall, in that same land

of reticulated caves,
a band of cells,
radiolaria-like, chromosome-like, germ-shapes seeding
the lens-fishes swimming in long meanders of sinusoidal

sun path,
centriole spindles tugging at the lens-ends, freefloating
4- and 5-fingered petal hands
trolling below, undergirding

the sea-band. Double axes
stabilize the quadrants
on the Grand Ellipse, the solar orbit: Solstice, Solstice;
Equinox, Equinox.

"We must seek," Simone said, "at greater depth
our own source,
for the Church destroyed Oc,"

the Occitanian world, a resisting tide, a river
of peoples in the honey-
combed caves near Toulouse, near Marseilles.
As electrons rush the tube

at one-fifth the speed of light, do they testify
to a prehistoric rupture,
a Glacial flood, or the dangerously close-coming
passage of the moon as Roadrunner boulders, meteorites

careen through the sky, crater the earth,
or was an inner sense of hearing-counting lost,
when the children stopped coming together
in a brood, in the easy spring, conceived at Midsummer,

and began to be born *throughout* the year, whenever.
And began to be garnered as workers
in a settling world. Their,

now unpredictable, mothers
no longer wander.
Someone has seen—
Who but I, says the bird.

And it flies away.
Renewal
assumed
to the ranking ladder and ranked below power,

ownership, fixed place, Force, to enforce.
"Pure gold, not alchemist's gold . . . but the true metal
dug out from mines where dragons stand watch."
Viète Isagoge, 1591. "He is referring,"

says André Weil, Simone's
brother, "to the power and scope of the new algebra.
The ore is from Diophantus."

Screech owl nailed to the barnhouse door,
blows raining down on her,
fagots heaped. The persecutor's desire
to see,

as he sets the ordeal. What has happened? All
participate: sabbat.
Freud to Fleiss, 1897, is speaking about
The Witch Fixer, Hexenhammer,

in Latin, *Malleus Maleficarum,* the work of two monks,
themselves German. "The medieval theory
of possession," Freud writes, "upheld by ecclesiastical
tribunals is identical to our theory . . .

why do confessions extorted by torture bear so
much resemblance to my
patients' narratives during treatment?" A plaintive

tone, as in
"Procne is among the slaves," that embroidered text
of a woman raped and her tongue cut out
by her brother-in-law. She is trying to address

her sister. And does. And they serve him
his child for dinner. And turn into birds.
Blank birds, they blend—into one name, Philomel.
Medieval story of the nightingale,

pressing her breast onto thorns, who can't remember
why she mourns. A real witch doesn't cry,
a real witch can't float.
Weight her down, if she drowns, you were correct

in your suspicions. Someone,
somewhere, saw, once, for the first time,
a rape, but which of them knew it?

"When the woman stays silent, it is
a grave sign,
also absence of tears." *MM (HH, The Witch Fixer).*
Water for the body,

language for the heart, found with the woman
of another tribe drawing at the well, with the water bird.
The woman who fails to inhibit her speech,
who can't stop talking, who can't stop bleeding,

an issue of blood, who can't stop flowing,
who can't stop putting her hair to his feet,
drying his feet with her flowing hair,
who can't stop spending. Widow who seeks

the smallest mite, but not to save it, to save the Year,
to retrieve and give it, giving all.
Wise virgins, who know to expect and provide.

How *could* desire
outrun satisfaction? Who is constantly
solicited, never satisfied, driven, forced to it,
forced to instruct: an albatross

at his neck,
provocative bird, for aimless years
above his conquering ship, on motionless wings,
before it lit—or would have lit—on Ramirez Island

where it had taken off. An albatross
mates for life
and returns to nest. But when it lifts, it glides five years
on its motionless—now bloodied, flapping wings.

How to make nothing of something.
Don't take me amiss. I mean nothing
by it, I mean only lightness,

a zephyr, a lilt, evanescent
yielding,
I mean electronic.
The ore is from Diophantus.

"The idea is to form the algebra of sections
of the bundle over the leaf space.
[Gap] . . . closed currents
on the space of leaves . . . a new technique— . . . to . . . reach

below the Planck scale and attempt to decipher
the fine structure
of space-time." *Notices of the AMS*, August
1997.

On "Kung Fu:
The Legend Continues," I learn to fear
the carved green phallus

covered with a dark cloth. Quivering bolts
leap to its beak, hiss intermittently,
attract, leach; but I'm taught to respect
the carved green chalice

protected by transparence;
though I cannot imagine
how to lift it, as Caine can, I drift inside it,
the low, flat, deep, full-footed bowl of figured mineral,

bone, horn, filigreed, veined with dark.
A complex message can pass only between
—emanation and absorption—
complexities of structure. In crystals

and organisms, resonant feedback
is required. Encounters of a special, precarious
sort. To claim a sense of company that survives

the loss of friends. To be vetted by
an Archaic
smile, by the kindness of strangers, a hazel nut,
the Duke o' Norroway, or a water bird.

A knowledge unsupported
by community, language, gender: a deep
exclusion, taking refuge, remembering
ordeal. His need to see. Remembering

burning. And communion in a garret.
A vision which ends, "I must withdraw,"
some sentences after
being thrown out.

Terror trapped in muscle cells.
Locked jaw, gritted teeth. A seeker
of perfection: once ravished, twice chaste.

Some see the strong *fiat* as hopelessly strong
and steel their mind to it.
Some see nothing, happenstance, confusion.
At the quantum, basis of all that is stable,

numeric and morphic play with each other.
Not whether, but when: each level within
the atom, a pattern of resonant lock—
and each one without.

Hard steel punch. Soft silver being chased.
Everything you taste, or hear, or touch,
has a kind of limit, in response to stress,
beyond which relaxation is . . . to . . . something

other.
Loss of core memory.
Erasure.

"Without this there would be no histor[y, no]
individuality in complex structures,"
says Smith, in *The Search for Structure*, MIT Press.
Is Heaven, then,

the never failing pattern, the refrain
that cannot stop?
If for history to come,
it must destruct,

how
good could Memory be?
That swell of breakage, torn tissue
of threads,

tangle adrift, ends
to pull. Is it taken on to make us?
By whom?

By what?
Vacuum fluctuation? Water Witch Wings?
A blushing whole?
Some would say shame

at such Fullness, a.k.a.
Emptiness, would motivate an act of defloration.
Some would say,
love leads to decreation, Simone's word, the putting away

of power, laying it aside, in a free
act of bittersweet removal, as
the Duke
in *Measure for Measure.*

The singularities of an automorphic
function are, if not a circle, a Cantor dust,
defusing the ancient paradox,

divisible without end but not continuous.
The infinitely thin
curtains swept back and back of a Cantor dust
"that seem to correspond

to a very deep
reality." Mathematicians
pen that stuff.
Minute portions of the world precisely as complex

and organized as the large.
Misfits may form
completely independent patterns
of their own, as beats in music,

or moiré in silk.
No equilibrium, when any *memory* of the previous
—vestige, remnant, trace, or ray—retained.

If we understood red, her web
blocking the path, glistening in sun, as the strong
door to dust, as a form
of strong transparence,

protecting the chalice, the bear, the canting horn,
filigreed, veined with dark.
Fear in the nursery.
Uninvited guest.

A spindle gift.
A child sleeps for a hundred years
behind the briar hedge.
One prick of blood.

What does matter about the function
is the nature of the peak
at its very center. Green and graceful witch,

inland woman who took the fury out
of the sea, (dis)solved in time, true, Mab has been
with thee, Mer Medb, Guinevere,
Finnabair, take off your shoes, spout

and prune, "do
while" the arc lasts in the sky—a double
positive is
not

a negative. "Yeah,
yeah."
☺ Deep
rule(s), par-t[ur]i-tion.

The delicacy
of fractal curves, point jumping
in the phase space,

tracery of frost on glass.
Any
section of such blown up—equally
exquisite, detailed, ever, over and over, a never

ending,
never decaying, never
exactly
the same pattern—recognizable at once.

Begin with a closed interval, include ends,
take out the middle: on the separated them, do
again, again . . . creating, or leaving, a structure more and more
open, of sparkling points.

Indra's Net? Cantor dust.
Do there exist beings where all take each other
into account, in their very core?

The smallest particles.
Renormalized photons.
List. I say *list*, that long implicit, blurred string
my mother

left me.
Isomorphism, another name for coding.
Words of others.
Lists and strings are fluid data structures.

The Glacier, calving, enormous roar
into a gray silent sea,
turquoise
lining.

Krill stains the snow
and the breasts of the penguins.
$\frac{1}{10}^{th}$ of a second,

the time it takes
to recognize your mother.
From one hundred million
retinal dots

to one
word
—*is it really*
you

I long to say?
Skim and teeter
of a moving balance, her beret,
Simone's,

as she stands
at prayer, very
slightly

swaying—swaying in the air
above her,
an emerald darner
hovers;

that, I think, she hears, but
does not see.

Divine Horsemen: The Living Gods of Haiti, Maya Deren, for Erzulie, Erzulie Ge-Rouge.

Fractals: Form, Chance and Dimension, Benoit Mandelbrot, for Cantor dusts. *The Fractal Geometry of Nature*, Benoit Mandelbrot, for Cantor dusts differently.

Hamlet's Mill: An Essay on Myth and the Frame of Time, Hertha von Dechend and Giorgio de Santillana, for precession of the equinoxes and, implicitly, Tarot.

"Ice Age Numbers," Arthur Corwin, in *Numbers, Exhibition Catalog*, The Cooper Union, October 4–26, 1989, for an eccentric view. Even better, Corwin's lectures, occasionally given, not yet committed to print, on Tarot and visual reading.

The Language of the Goddess, Marija Gimbutas, for Çatal Hüyük, bull gods, V's, M's, waterbirds, and the like.

Notebooks, Simone Weil, for her wide-ranging views.

Notices of the American Mathematical Society, August 1997, for partisan expositions of Alain Connes's *Noncommutative Geometry*.